SO-AKM-246

BOOK 1

# Polly Diamond
## and the Magic Book

Alice Kuipers

Diana Toledano

SCHOLASTIC INC.

The author would like to thank Karen
for her help and encouragement, and Ayden for
the inspiration. Thank you, thank you.

No part of this publication may be reproduced, stored in a retrieval system, or transmitted in any form or by any means, electronic, mechanical, photocopying, recording, or otherwise, without written permission of the publisher. For information regarding permission, write to Chronicle Books LLC, 680 Second Street, San Francisco, CA 94107.

ISBN 978-1-338-55128-0

Text copyright © 2018 by Alice Kuipers. Illustrations copyright © 2018 by Diana Toledano. All rights reserved. Published by Scholastic Inc., 557 Broadway, New York, NY 10012, by arrangement with Chronicle Books LLC. SCHOLASTIC and associated logos are trademarks and/or registered trademarks of Scholastic Inc.

The publisher does not have any control over and does not assume any responsibility for author or third-party websites or their content.

12 11 10 9 8 7 6 5 4 3 2 1                    19 20 21 22 23 24

Printed in the U.S.A.                         23

First Scholastic printing, February 2019

Design by Sara Gillingham Studio
Typeset in Chaparral and Nouveau Crayon

For my daughter, Lola,
with all my love. A. K.

For my parents,
because they always made
room for more books in our
tiny home. D. T.

# ONE

Today something amazing is going to happen.

Amazing things always happen in threes.

Day One: On Friday, my teacher, Ms. Hairball, told me my color poem was fantastic.

Day Two: On Saturday, my pet rock, Stoneface, smiled at me. I saw him! I swear!

Today is Sunday. Day Three.

So yes. Today is going to be amazing. Super-fantastic. I start a list on a blank sheet of paper. I love writing lists.

# To-Do List for a Super-Fantastic Day
## BY POLLY DIAMOND

---

- Write a story
- Paint my bedroom
- Discover a secret treasure
- Travel somewhere no one has ever been

More than writing lists, I love writing stories.

## A Story About a Perfect House
### BY POLLY DIAMOND

My house is too teeny. My parents say it's cozy. But it's NOT. Our house is stuffed full. Our house probably feels like it has eaten too much food!

*Burp*

AND we have a new baby coming any day. When he comes, the house will be even more stuffed. Mom says Anna and I have to share a room now.

So we have a room for the baby. Yuck.

We need a bigger house. We need lots of rooms. A perfect house would—

I hear a drumroll and a trumpet blast at the front door.

Everyone says I'm imaginative. But I definitely heard a drumroll and a trumpet blast.

Maybe it's a caterpillar army on the march.

Or a hedgehog band.

Or an armadillo performing a circus trick. Yes, that's it. An armadillo.

I run to open the door.

It's WAY BETTER than an armadillo. It's a package!

I pick it up. It's hard, thin, and flat. It's wrapped in pretty polka-dot paper. In the corner a gold stamp reads: **Special Delivery from the Writing and Spelling Department**. Below that, in letters as bubbly as clouds, it says:

# FOR POLLY DIAMOND

My heart skips rope. I rip open the wrapping.
Inside is a turquoise leather book. Turquoise! The best!
My glasses are turquoise. My sneakers are
turquoise. My favorite pen is turquoise. Also, not
everyone can spell TURQUOISE. But I can. I love
words that are hard to spell.

I open the book.

## A WRITING AND SPELLING BOOK FOR POLLY DIAMOND

I wish my writing looked like that. Mine is as messy as my bedroom.

I flip through the rest of the book. All the other pages are blank.

Back in the kitchen I hunt for my pen. I'm always looking for my stuff! I wonder if sometimes my things scurry around the house like busy mice.

Where *is* my pen? A-HA!

I slide it from behind my ear.

As I write, I try to make my letters as neat as possible:

This book belongs to Polly Diamond.

Whoa! A bizarre, baffling thing happens. Under my name, a tiny black dot pops onto the page.

Slowly, the dot moves. *All by itself.*

It becomes the letter **H**.

I touch it. As I take away my finger, another letter appears.

An **E**.

An **L** is next.

Then another **L**.

Then an **O**.

Then, like a sprinter rushing to finish the race, it spells my name followed by an exclamation mark**!**

**HELLO, Polly Diamond!**

The book is writing back to me!

# TWO

"Polly?" Mom calls from
upstairs. "Could you come
and help Anna?"

I hear Anna yell, "No! No!
No!" She is three and a half.

"In one teeny minute," I yell
back. I run my finger over the
words: **HELLO, Polly Diamond!**

The book writes: **Stop! That tickles!**

I'm woozy (*woozy* is one of my favorite words. I love words with double letters in them). I'm dizzy (double *zz*!)! I wonder if I might faint. I've always wondered what fainting would feel like.

But I don't faint. Instead, I write: How do you do that?

**Do what?**

Write back to me.

**I'm a writing and spelling book. That's what I do! Do you like to write, too?**

Everything! Stories! Lists!

**Like what?**

Like this:

# Top Names to Call My New Baby Brother

- Darwin
- Fernando
- Gill
- Edgar
- Basile

That's my favorite
so far. Basile It's
the name of an
herb and a person.
I love words that mean more than one
thing. But really, I love all words.

**I love words, too!**

Can you think of any more names?

**How about . . .**

## Names NOT to Call Your New Baby Brother

- **Waldo**
- **Nightmare**
- **Rocket**
- **Banana**

I giggle. I add:

- Pilot
- Galaxy
- Honeybee

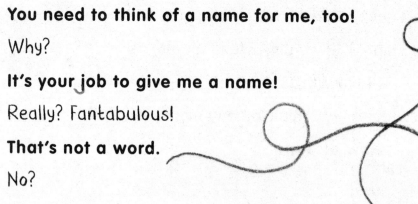

The book writes:

**You need to think of a name for me, too!**

Why?

**It's your job to give me a name!**

Really? Fantabulous!

**That's not a word.**

No?

"Polly, please!" Mom calls.

"Sorry, coming!"

I take my book with me. In the upstairs hallway,
I leap over a roll of carpet.
It's like a giant sleeping
snake. This
is a simile—
I learned about
similes from
Ms. Hairball. The carpet
is not *really* a giant
snake. It just *looks*
a lot like one.

I one-handed-cartwheel into Anna's old room. It smells of new paint: Sunbeam Yellow.

"Careful, Polly!" Mom cries.

Dad comes in, rubbing his eyes behind his glasses. He's still in his PJs.

"Hey, Polly D. I think your mom called you two thousand times." His feet look like hairy gorilla feet. This is not a simile. He is wearing his gorilla slippers.

"She called me *twice*," I say.

"She called you three billion times!" he jokes.

"Anna, this is not your room anymore," Mom says. Anna is jumping on the baby mattress on the floor. I can't believe I have to share a room with her. I make a list in my head.

## Ways to Get Anna Out of My Bedroom

- Tell her it's haunted
- Turn her into a pet rock
- Put a lock on the door
- Move her bed into a nearby river and watch it float away

Dad started putting together our old crib yesterday. He hasn't finished it. Bits of it are all over the floor. The curtains are on the floor, too. Along with a pile of new blue baby clothes that Granny sent.

Having a contractor dad means our house is ALWAYS under construction. When I was little, I thought his job was in DEstruction, not CONstruction, because he's always taking apart something in our house.

Mom rubs her huge tummy. I think about what the baby is doing in there. Maybe somersaults. Maybe he'll be an acrobat.

I imagine our family circus.

- Dad—clown
- Mom—ringmaster
- Anna—dancer
- Me—lion tamer

## Names for Our Family Circus

- The Dazzling Diamonds
- The Gem Stars
- The Jumping Jewels

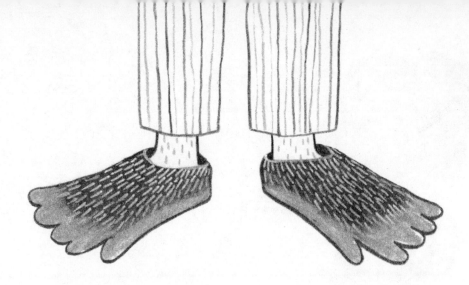

Dad wiggles his huge gorilla feet. "Take Anna downstairs, Polly Poppet."

"But I want to show you my new book. It writes back to me!"

Anna jumps over. "Can I see?"

"No. Do NOT touch it."

"Why don't you start making chocolate chip pancake batter?" Dad gently turns me toward the bedroom door. "I'll be down to help in a minute. We can look at your book then. Okay?"

"Yum! Okay. That's a deal."

Downstairs, I pull out Granny's recipe book. I love the smell of the old, yellow pages. I love her scribbled notes. I find her pancake recipe.

I open our cupboard.

Hmmm. We have no flour. But there is a can of baking powder. It looks exactly like flour. I dump the baking powder into a bowl. I crack one egg on top. I pick out the pieces of shell.

I tip in a cup of milk and stir the mix, which fizzes a bit. Then—the best part—I pour in chocolate chips.

Ta-da! Mmm! Maybe when I grow up, I can be a chef.

*"Welcome to Diamond's*

*Delicious Desserts,"* I sing. I love words that all begin with the same letter: amazing alliterations. I whip open my new book and write:

## Polly Diamond's New & Improved Chocolate Chip Pancakes:

- One cup of baking powder
- One egg
- One cup of milk
- Lots of chocolate chips
- Rainbow sprinkles to decorate
- A dollop of whipped cream

Dad comes into the kitchen. There is milk all over the counter and egg gunk on the floor. Somehow, Anna has gotten hold of the syrup bottle. Dad's eyebrows shoot up. "Wow, Polly, you sure went to town in here."

"It could be worse," I say. "I didn't spill any sprinkles."

"You clean up. I'll cook." He inspects the pancake mix. "Uh, Polly, did you follow the recipe?"

"We have no flour," I say. "I used baking powder instead."

"Baking-powder-tastic, Polly Parrot." He scoops my mix into the garbage. "I'll make it again." He turns to the cupboard. "Uh, Polly, what's this?"

I frown because on the shelf there is a full cup of what looks like baking powder. But the can of baking powder I used is already out on the counter. Next to the baking powder on the shelf is a cup of milk. And a dollop of whipped cream. An egg rolls out and smashes on the floor. Chocolate chips and rainbow sprinkles are *everywhere*.

Dad rubs his forehead as Mom waddles in like a penguin.

"*Miss* made a *mess*," Dad says to her. "Don't worry, love. We're just about to clean up."

"Refusing to worry. Refusing to look," Mom says, keeping her gaze on the ceiling. "Oh, no, I *looked*. I'm leaving right now."

"Sorry, Mom," I say. *Sorry* is always a useful word when Mom is frowning. I kiss Mom goodbye. I kiss Mom's huge tummy, too. "Bye, baby. I definitely think we should call you Gill. Or Basil. Basil is the top name on my list. It means an herb AND—"

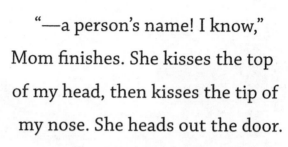

"—a person's name! I know," Mom finishes. She kisses the top of my head, then kisses the tip of my nose. She heads out the door.

I turn to Dad. "Can we do my bedroom today?"

"*My* bedroom!" Anna yells.

"If you clean up some of your stuff so I can reach the walls," Dad suggests. "Then we can paint. But first let's start in here."

I give him a huge hug. Then I begin to wipe up the mysterious messy mess in the cupboard.

# THREE

After breakfast, Dad makes a work call. It takes a thousand years. I decide to help him out. I've seen Dad paint hundreds of times. I find the two cans of paint in the upstairs closet. Along with rollers. And trays. But no ladder. I won't be able to reach the top of my walls.

The paint cans are HEAVY. I struggle along the walkway. I stumble over the roll of carpet. In my room, I heave the paint cans over the books that are stacked everywhere. I own three books about writing. And lots of storybooks.

## My Favorite Books

‿‿‿‿‿‿‿‿‿‿

- *Ivy and Bean*
- *Harry Potter and the Sorcerer's Stone*
- *The Doll People*
- *When Birds Could Talk & Bats Could Sing*
- *Juana & Lucas*
- *Captain Underpants*

I also have a library card. I borrow books about magic and faraway places and deep-sea diving. Maybe I will be a real-life treasure hunter one day.

I stare at Anna's side of the room.

Anna's pink dollhouse.

Anna's huge, pink stuffed unicorn.

Anna's
pile of pink
ruffled dresses.

Too. Much. Pink.

I can't believe I have
to share a room with The Sparkle
Princess.

But never mind. Time to get to work.

I need to move the furniture first. I push both beds away from the walls. I shove our toys and clothes into a mountain on top of them. I throw our quilts over everything to protect our things from paint spills. Then I take down photos of my friends and my artwork and shove them under the beds. Dad will be so pleased!

I take a break and flop onto my bed with my book. I write:

## A Painting Adventure
### BY POLLY DIAMOND

**I like the title!**

Thanks! It's a story about painting my room Aquarium Blue.

**That's the name of the paint? Paint gets a name?**

All sorts of names. Like Plum Crazy or Go Mango.

**Go Mango is not a real paint name! I bet I can think of sillier names for paint:**

- **Muddy Pond**
- **Lunch Bag**
- **Don't Lilac to Me**

I think for a minute. Then I write:

- Fungus Among Us
- **Baboon Butt?**

FINISH

GO, MANGO, GO!

I burst out laughing.

Then, I write: Oh, I have an idea for a story . . .

## Painting Day
### BY POLLY DIAMOND

Today is a painting day. I have paint and a
brush and I'm going to pile up the stacks of
books in my room like a ladder so I can reach
the high spots. When I—

A weird creaking comes from my floor. I look up. My *books* are drifting like small ships up from the rug. Then they hover, one above the other, creating steps between them—like a *ladder*.

My mouth drops open. I slide off my bed.

It's astonishing. It's astounding. It's astronomical!

I grab my new book and write:
How did that happen???
**That's what I do!**

I flip to the recipe I wrote. A brilliant idea jiggles in my mind. I remember the piles of chocolate chips in the kitchen cupboard. My new book made them appear! And the milk. And the sprinkles. Because of the words *I* wrote.

This is awesome! I'm so gonna use this ladder to paint my room right now!

I toss my new book onto my bed. I open a paint can with Dad's screwdriver.

Then I stir the paint with a ruler and I dip in a brush. I slosh paint over my fingers.

I test the book ladder with the tip of my toe. When I push my foot down, the book dips just a little. I put a little more weight on it. The book dips a tiny bit more, but holds steady. I step onto it. It is very wobbly. I accidentally splosh paint on Anna's pink ballerina quilt.

Then an idea bursts in my head like a firework. I can't believe I didn't think of it right away! I jump off the ladder, spilling more paint.

I write: The walls of my bedroom are painted Aquarium Blue, like an aquarium!

Dad calls from downstairs. "Polly?"

I drop my brush and make a quick stop in the bathroom to wash the paint off my hands. I slide down the banister, holding my brilliant book tight.

In the kitchen, Dad is still on the phone.

"Can you play with Anna?" he asks. "It's your mom calling."

"I wanna play hide-and-seek." Anna pulls my leg. Her hair is tangled. Her clothes are covered in glitter.

"I'll hide," I say to Anna. "Go count. NO PEEKING."

I duck under the table with my magic book. I watch Dad's gorilla feet go by. He is talking excitedly on the phone. I listen to Anna calling for me.

I write:

# The Top Reason Why I Love
# to Play Hide-and-Seek

eeeeeeeee

I feel like I'm invisible, and I love it!

## Invisible? Cool!

Dad gets off the phone. "Polly, where are you?"

"I can't find her ANYWHERE!" Anna says.

"Polly!" Dad's gorilla feet go by again. "Come out, come out, wherever you are. Exciting news! Our new baby is coming."

I scramble out from under the table.

Dad pushes his hands into his hair so it sticks up. "Polly?" he calls.

I step right in front of him.

"Polly? Where *are* you?"

"Dad, I'm here," I say. I giggle because he is looking *right at me*.

"Not funny, Polly." His voice is sharp. He looks over his shoulder—as if I might be behind him. "Where are you?"

I think about what I just wrote.

Dad interrupts my thinking. His voice is loud as he makes another call.

"Hi, Lori?" he says. "It's time!"

My heart floats like a balloon. Lori Arbul is Mom's best friend. They've been best friends for a thousand years. She is also my teacher.

Ms. Hairball is coming over! The baby is coming!

And I am invisible!!!

# FOUR

## The Best Things About Ms. Hairball

• Ms. Hairball is a *published* author. We have
copies of her two books in our classroom.
One book is called *Flat Earth Theory*. It's
about a girl who is certain the world is flat.
It's really funny.

- Ms. Hairball has a voice that is sweet and soft, like marshmallows. I could listen to her all day. I could eat marshmallows all day, too.
- Ms. Hairball is small and round, like an apple. Even her hair is red.
- Ms. Hairball loves cats, photographs, and traveling—she sends cool postcards to us from all over the world. And she loves turquoise!

I could go on forever, but Dad calls out, "Polly, Shaylene is coming first. Lori will get here as soon as she can."

My balloon
heart pops.
Shaylene? *Blerk.*
Shaylene is
Ms. Hairball's niece.
She's fourteen. She thinks she's a model.
She is the worst babysitter ever. But
she babysits us all the time because my
parents love her. So does every grown-up
in Utopia. (That's the town where I live.
*Utopia* means *perfect place*, which it is, if
you mean PERFECT-ly ordinary.)

Dad hunts for his keys. Like me, Dad
is always looking for his stuff. I spot the
keys on the counter. I pick them up, and
they look as though they are floating. I
jangle them.

Dad doesn't even notice that the keys are floating. He must really be focused on Mom and the new baby!

Shaylene comes in the front door. Today her hair is blue.

"Hel-looo-oooo," she calls. Even her voice is annoying. "You must be sooooooo excited, Mr. Diamond."

I drop Dad's keys into his pocket.

"Oh, there they are," he says, a bit confused. "Polly? Where are you? I have to go. Okay. I love you, Amazing Anna." He grabs Anna and squeezes her tight. "Love you, too, Dolly P, wherever you are!" he yells. He rushes out the door wearing his gorilla slippers!

As soon as he's gone, Shaylene says, "Okay, kidlets, let's hope I'm not stuck here all day."

## An Endless List of Annoying Things About Shaylene

- She calls us kidlets.
- She changes her hair color every week. Which is cool. But then she talks about her hair all the time.
- She's always looking at her phone. Or talking on her phone. Or taking selfies.
- She tells me often that when I was a baby, I had stinky poopy diapers.

"Play with me!" Anna orders Shaylene.

"Go play with Polly," Shaylene says. "Where is she?"

"I'm here!"

Anna jerks her head in my direction.

"Don't be scared," I whisper in her ear. "I'm just invisible."

"Where are you, Polly?" Shaylene calls out.

"She's invisible," Anna says. For a three-and-a-half-year-old, she's much smarter than Shaylene.

Shaylene turns to Anna. "I see," she says.

I giggle because Shaylene doesn't *see* at all!

Then I hear a splashy-sploshy noise. Like water. And a flippy-floppy noise. Like a fish.

It's coming from *my bedroom*.

I race upstairs and push open my bedroom door. Then I slam it shut behind me!

My bedroom walls look WET. They shimmer. But there is not a drip anywhere. And REAL fish swim along the walls. Seaweed sways by the windows. Coral glows in the corners. The room looks like an aquarium.

I spread out my arms. I spin around. Fish flash past. Big ones. Tiny ones. Yellow ones. Purple ones.

A crab scuttles along the baseboard.

I open my book and write:

You turned my room into a *real* aquarium!

**Do you like it?**

I love it! What else can you do?

**Anything you can imagine. You just have to write it down.**

Ideas fizz into my head like bubbles in soda pop.

- Heaps of chocolate
- A cell phone
- A bigger house
- My own bedroom
- More books
- A flat-screen TV
- A four-poster bed
- A waterslide
- A horse
- A dragon
- To go to the moon
- Or Mars.
- Or Hogwarts.

Yikes! This list could get really long! Then in my head, Mom says: *Tell me something kind you did today.* Hmm. I think. I think a little more. Then I write:

I wish for world peace.

I fill up with happiness at how kind and thoughtful I am.

**Polly?**

I imagine a world with no war. Everyone would smile all the time. And, of course, everyone would be very grateful to me, Polly Diamond. I imagine getting a big award.

**Polly?**

What?

**I can't make world peace happen.**

The image of me shaking the president's hand bursts.

I start to write: How about a—

But the door swings open. Anna stomps in. "Polly! Where are you?"

"Don't you remember the rule?" I say.

"No." She scampers around my room like an excited puppy. "Pretty fishies."

"You have to knock before you come in."

"It's *my* room, too. You have to share!" She reaches for a yellow fish.

"Don't touch anything," I say.

She snatches the yellow fish. FROM THE WALL. It flops out of her hand, like a bar of soap in the bath. The fish lies, gasping on the floor. Its mouth pops open and shut.

"Look what you've done!" I run over and pick up the fish. It shoots from my hand toward the watery wall. It swims into the shimmering blue.

Anna reaches for a striped fish.

"Stop it, Anna!"

"No," she says. "I'm a mermaid."

"You're not a mermaid. But I'll turn you into a—
into a—a banana if you're not careful." I grab my book.

She dives for a
fish. It darts away.
Quickly, I write:
Anna is a banana.
There's a *POP*! And then
lying on the floor is a banana.
A perfect, yellow banana.

# FIVE

My sister is a banana! That's bananas!

"Kidlets, where are you?" Shaylene yells from downstairs.

I pick up the banana. In my invisible hand, it—she?—looks as though it (she?) is hovering in the air. I carry it and my book downstairs.

Shaylene is busy texting. I wave Anna the Banana in front of her. Shaylene is going to freak out when she sees a hovering banana! She will think there is a ghost in the house!

She flicks at her phone's screen. She is amazingly unobservant. (I love how adding *un-* to the front of a word gives it the opposite meaning.)

I put the banana on the kitchen counter. I pick up Anna's toy T. rex. I roar.

Shaylene starts to look up. Then her phone blasts its annoying ringtone: it's her own voice saying *pickuppickuppickuppickup.*

"I have to babysit.
BOOOOORRRRINGGG,"
she says into her phone.

I make the T. rex roar
again.

She keeps chatting.

I put the T. rex down
and stick my invisible tongue
out at Shaylene.

Mom sometimes says: *Always know when
to quit.* Dad normally replies: *Never give up!*

Shaylene snorts into her phone.

I shake my head at her. Sadly. Even sorrow-
FULLY! (I like how adding the word *fully* to the
end of a word makes it even bigger. Bigger, bigger,
bigger.) Suddenly, I remember how much I want a
bigger house! I open my magic book. I write:

# My Perfect House

My house is perfectly palatial. (Two *P* words!)
It has a lot of rooms so Anna and I don't
have to share anymore. (Although now that
she's a banana, she doesn't take up much
space.) One room has a dance studio with
tutus, beanbags, pom-poms, and
rhythm sticks (for Anna). Or
maybe not. Bananas can't
dance! There is a game room with
board games, card games, and video
games. One room is for
crafts, with paper, stencils,
stickers, pipe cleaners,
glitter glue, and

paints. A swimming pool is filled with floating toys!

There is a spiral staircase. And there are birds on the wallpaper along the stairs (for Mom—she loves birds).

There are loads of books (for all of us).

My room has a bed fit for a queen.

There is a waterslide (for me).

Oh, and the roll of carpet in the hallway is—

I think for a second. What do people do with carpet? Stick it? Fix it? I write:

—fixed up.

That's about right. Anyway, my book will know what I mean. I'm about to write more. But the house begins to tremble. It's like an earthquake.

My glasses fall off. The floor beneath me shakes harder. I fall to my knees. I feel like I'm in a blender. Shake, shake, shake. I can't open my mouth to yell. Not that anyone could hear me over the rumbling.

There is a ripping sound. Like a giant pair of jeans is being torn apart.

Then the house stops shaking. And everything is very quiet.

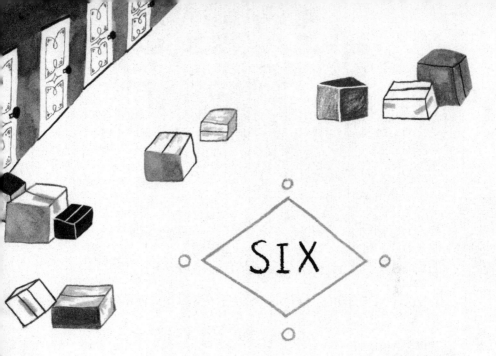

# SIX

I fumble for my glasses. The whole house is completely changed!

The hallway is the *longest* I've ever seen. I'm not sure I can spot the end of it, even when I squint. There are hundreds of doors. Thousands of doors. Maybe a million doors. Stacked along the walls are a gazillion boxes. They are like large toy blocks scattered by a giant baby.

The roll of carpet is stuck to the ceiling!

I write: Double, triple awesome! But why is the carpet on the ceiling?

**You wrote, The roll of carpet in the hallway is fixed up.**

But I didn't mean . . . never mind! It doesn't matter! I can't wait to see what's inside all the boxes!

I open a box. It's jam-packed full of books. I open another one. Same thing. More books. I open five or six more boxes. Each box is full of books.

Fantabulous!

I turn to the squillions of doors.

I imagine I'm an explorer. I can see the news headline:

# INTREPID AND DARING EXPLORER
## POLLY DIAMOND,
### DISCOVERER OF UNMAPPED OCEANS AND UNKNOWN ISLANDS

Today Polly Diamond, the bravest explorer ever, will explore what is behind each of the squillion doors.

I push a door, but it's stuck. I shove harder. It opens a crack. Bottles tumble out.

I go to the next door. And the next. There are three libraries jammed with even *more* books. I pause at a dance studio, which is loaded with tutus and pink shoes. I shut that door. I do NOT like ballet. Or pink. Another room is stuffed full of art supplies.

I push open door after door. And door after door. After door.

Then I see a SWIMMING POOL. It is so full of rubber ducks and inner tubes and inflatable dolphins that it would be impossible to swim in it!

I find a spiral staircase and slide down the banister from fantastic floor to fabulous floor.

Along the stairs the wallpaper has bird pictures. But the birds *move*. They twitter and tweet. They fluff their wings. Finally, I open a turquoise door.

*tweet*

It's my bedroom! The fish are still swimming along the walls. But now in the middle is a round *twelve*-poster bed. It looks like a crown. I leap onto the bed. OUCH! It's very hard! As hard and as pretty as a crown.

And there is a waterslide! I climb to the top. I whiz down. But it doesn't get me wet. I go up and down ten times. Twenty.

There is a huge flat-screen TV on my wall. I stop sliding and flick through the channels. I flip open

my book and write: Thank you—I love the new house. It's perfect!

**I am glad you like it!**

Actually, you know what? There are a couple of extra things we could do.

**Really? Like what?**

I tap my pen against my tongue. Ideas float around my head. I could write about a beach in the yard and a chocolate fountain in every room.

My tummy growls. I'm so hungry, I could eat a cat. (That's my dad's way of saying he's SUPER hungry. Ms. Hairball says this is called *hyperbole*. This means Dad is exaggerating. Eating a cat would be *disgusting*.)

I write: We can work more on the house later. First, can I have a sandwich, please? Not peanut butter. I do NOT like peanut butter! Hmmm . . . Can I have a club sandwich?

**Sure.**

Next to me on the bed pops a very large plate. On it are two slices of buttered bread. Both are stuck to the sides of a *wooden bat.* What is *that?*

**A club sandwich. It's what *you* wrote! A *club* sandwich. Definition of club: a heavy stick with a thick end.**

I giggle. Mom sometimes says: *You get what you get, and you don't get upset.* It's so rhymey, it *must* be true.

I write: Believe me, that's not a club sandwich.
A club sandwich is—

**I got it. My mistake!**

Another plate pops onto my bed. On it is a thin
sandwich. I inspect it. Between the slices of bread
is a buttery playing card. An ace. The ace of clubs! I
start laughing.

I write: Not that kind of club, either!

**What, then? You mean like a
group of *people*? People on a
sandwich?**

Never mind!
I'll go make
*myself* something
to eat.

# SEVEN

A looooong time later, I'm still looking for the kitchen. I've opened so many doors that my arm hurts. My tummy grumbles. I'm so hungry, I could eat a horse. An elephant. Two elephants.

I hear Shaylene calling, "Polly? Anna? Where are you?"

Shaylene! Anna! I forgot all about them.

I run toward Shaylene's voice. It's faint. She's down one floor from me, I think.

Each step of the staircase plays a musical note as I run down. I want to run up and down to play a song. But Shaylene yells again, "Polly, where are you?"

I follow her voice through a door. It's the kitchen! A shiny new kitchen full of boxes. Shaylene is sitting on the floor, rubbing her head.

"Are you okay?" I ask, climbing over a box.

She screams like a thousand bees are stinging her. She jumps up. "Oh, no! Oh, no!" she yells. "I'm going crazy. I'm crazy. Where am I? Where are the kidlets? Who is talking?"

Oh, right. I'm invisible!

"Shaylene, it's me!" I say.

She spins around and trips over a box. She lands on the floor again. She grabs her phone. And presses 9-1—

"No!" I snatch the phone.

She screams again.

"Stop yelling! It's me! Polly!" I wave the phone around.

"I must have really banged my head," she says.

"Do you want some chocolate?" I ask.

She giggles. "A flying phone asking if I want chocolate." Her voice is a bit dreamy, as if she's half asleep. She rubs her head. "I *am* hungry. But I'm on a diet." She gets up and reaches across the counter.

She reaches for a banana.

But not just any banana.

She reaches for Anna the Banana.

I imagine myself leaping across the room. I imagine kicking the banana from Shaylene's hand.

Sadly, I'm not a very good leap-kicker. Instead I shout, "STOP! DON'T TOUCH THE BANANA!"

"Okay, okay," she says, rubbing her head. "I'm putting down the banana."

I hurry over and take Anna the Banana.

Shaylene blinks and looks around. She mumbles to herself, "Whoa. The kitchen looks different. Major renovations!"

I look at the huge, shiny kitchen with its zillions of cupboards.

I think about the squillions of rooms. The billions of boxes.

"This place is too crazy," Shaylene says.

She's right. It is.

"No problem! I'll fix it," I say.

I put Anna into the fruit bowl. Then I pull out my book and write: The house is like it used to be.

The house shakes and rumbles. With one hand, I hold on to my glasses. With the other, I hold on to the counter.

The cabinets crackle and burst like popcorn. The floor warps and reshapes. Shaylene stares with big, round eyes. Then she says "Whaaaaat?" and faints. The house stops shaking.

I look around the kitchen. But it's not *our* kitchen. I've *never* seen this room before. The floor is like a chessboard, black and white. The walls are mint-green. An old-fashioned pair of chairs and a small table are in the middle.

A family photograph hangs on the wall. But it's *not* our family. The photograph is black-and-white. In it are two kids, a mom wearing an old-fashioned dress, and a dad in a suit. *Who are these people?*

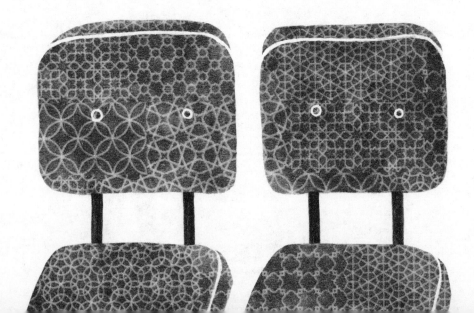

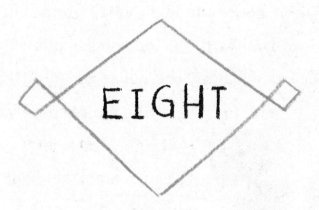

# EIGHT

This is not *our* kitchen. I read over what I wrote. *The house is like it used to be.*

I look around the kitchen. My brain *tick, tick, ticks*. Then, *DING*! It feels like an alarm clock is ringing in my head. I write in my book: When I wrote how the kitchen *used to be*, I meant earlier today. Not how it used to be in the past, before we lived here! We have to fix this. Right now.

**How?**

I want the house to go back.

The whole house shudders, creaks, and shifts. It *moves* toward our yard. The walls shake. Boxes topple.

STOP! I don't want the house to go backward!

The house stops moving. I sigh with relief. I write:

I just want my house to be normal.

I think about the word *normal.*

The house is beginning to shudder and rumble.

NO! STOP! Not *normal.* I don't want a normal, everyday house. I just want *our* house.

**Okay. I'm ready when you are.**

Wait! Let me think.

I take a deep breath.

I am a very good writer.

I can do this.

Using my imagination, I start at the bottom of my house and work my way to the top.

Then, using my turquoise pen, I start to write.

I use my best words to describe our house. Like *cozy*. And *stuccoed*. And *timbered* (which is the word

Dad uses to describe

the outside of our house).

I think about writing *rabbit warren*. But I decide

NOT to use it to describe my house. My book might

fill my house with rabbits! I decide to save rabbit

warren for another story, another day.

I write my bedroom back with all my books. I

write about Anna's pink, glittery bedcover and all

her stuffed animals. I describe my parents' room.

I put in Mom's dresser with all her makeup lined
neatly on top. I write in the baby's room, even the
crib in bits on the floor. I put in every single detail.
When I've finished, I title it:

## OUR WARM, COZY, LOVING HOME

Then I remember one last thing.

And I, Polly Diamond, am not invisible.

**Are you sure? Being invisible is pretty awesome.**

I consider it. Being invisible is totally awesome.
But I bet Mom won't let me hold my baby brother if
she can't *see* me.

I'm sure.

**Anything else?**

I think.

Oh, all right. Anna's not a banana anymore.
She's just Anna.

The walls begin to rumble and shake.

# NINE

When the rumbling stops, Shaylene sits up and rubs her head. "Polly!" she says. "What's going on?" She looks around nervously.

"I'm hungry," Anna says.

"Do you want a banana?" I offer. And giggle.

"Hello, everyone! Where are you?" Ms. Hairball calls in her soft, sweet voice from the front door.

We hurry into the hallway.

"Guess what?" Ms. Hairball takes off her flowery coat.

I'm too busy looking around the house to answer. Phew! Everything is perfect! I even remembered that the picture by the front door is of a horse. I really am a very good writer. It's our regular house. I glance up the stairs. The carpet is not on the ceiling anymore! But the roll of carpet isn't on the floor, either. Whoops. I must have forgotten to write it in.

Shaylene comes up behind me. She puts her hand on my shoulder. "Is Anna still a banana?" she asks quietly.

"A what?" Ms. Hairball asks. "What's going on?"

"I was a banana!" Anna says. "Polly was invisible!"

"I have a magic book," I say. "Everything I write comes true."

"A banana, huh! How fun," says Ms. Hairball. "I'm glad you've had a good time."

"The house had thousands of rooms," I say. "And Anna really was a banana."

"Any guesses yet?" Ms. Hairball asks. "Your parents have exciting news!"

"What?" I ask.

"Your brother arrived!"

"Our brother?" I say. My *brother*. My new baby brother.

"Look!" Ms. Hairball holds up a photo on her phone. The baby is small and scrunched.

"Yuck," says Anna.

"He's soooooo cute!" Shaylene cries.

I roll my eyes. Like Anna, I have a scary-good eye roll. Secretly, I agree with Anna. The baby looks like a big raisin.

"What's his name? *Cootchie-cooooo*," Shaylene says to the photo.

"Finn," Ms. Hairball replies.

"Finn? Like a shark fin? That was *not* on my list," I say.

"Shall we call your parents, girls?"

When Dad answers the phone, I say, "I like the name Finn, but I like the name Basil better."

"That's good," Dad says, "because his name is Finn Basil Diamond."

"Seriously?"

"Seriously," he says.

"It's the best name ever."

"How's everything at your end?"

"Great!" I say. "I turned the house into a house with a thousand rooms. My bedroom was an aquarium."

"*Super-Polly-tastic*," says Dad.

"I really did!"

In the background at his end, there's a LOUD yell.

"Is that baby Basil?" I ask.

"*Finn* is very . . . vocal about what he wants," Dad replies. "You wanna talk to Mom?"

Finn gets even louder.

"Maybe later," I say.

"Good idea," says Dad. "Okay, Dolly P. See you in the morning. And then you can show me your book."

My tummy grumbles.

"I'm so hungry," I say to Ms. Hairball as I hand the phone to Anna.

"Let's eat," says Ms. Hairball.

"After we eat," I say, "maybe we can fix up the house for baby Basil."

"Fix up the house?" repeats Shaylene, turning away from her phone. Her eyebrows rise.

I imagine my house fixed *up*. Perhaps my book would put it in the sky! "Actually, I probably don't want to fix it *up*! But don't worry," I say. "I have a great idea."

After supper, we get to work. Shaylene and Ms. Hairball put up the curtains. They're patterned with birds. I smooth on the wall stickers.

Shaylene checks her phone. "Nooooooo way! A giant snake was just captured on Main Street."

"A giant snake?" I say. "Was it as big as . . . oh . . . I don't know—a roll of carpet?"

"Snakes are gross!" cries Shaylene, still looking at her phone. She passes me a onesie. We all take the tags off the baby clothes. Ms. Hairball strings up some fairy lights that we find in the basement.

"Baby Finn needs fish," Anna says, looking at the walls.

I giggle. A fin needs a fish! "But our fish are gone," I say. "Maybe when Dad's back, we can paint our room Aquarium Blue. Like an aquarium."

"Okay," she says. She picks up her stuffed unicorn and puts it in the baby's crib. "Our baby can have that."

"I'm glad you're not a banana anymore," I say.

"Me, too."

I notice my open book on the floor. It has written to me: **So, have you picked out my name?**

Your name? I forgot I was supposed to give you a name! Hmmm. What about Mint? Mint is a great name. *Mint* means an herb—like Basil—AND *mint* means a place where money is made, AND it means new and unused, AND it's a word for candy.

**Um . . . any other ideas?**

Crane? That's the name of a machine and a bird. Or Jam—a thing to eat, and a word for when people squeeze together, and a word for when a band plays. Or Date—a fruit, and an outing . . .

**Those aren't really names.**

I think. And think. And think
some more. Then I smile.

So, have you picked out my name?

SPELL. It means three things—a spell, like a short period of time. But that's not the best meaning. It means *spell*, like a magic spell, AND *spell*, like spelling a word! You are a writing and spelling book after all!

**My name's Spell! I love it!**

What should we do tomorrow, Spell?

**Whatever you like.**

Spell's right. We can do *whatever* we like together.

"Kidlets, come on," interrupts Shaylene. "We're nearly done in here."

I put the book to one side and draw a picture of our whole family on paper Ms. Hairball gave me. I draw baby Finn Basil Diamond in the center. I color. Anna covers the edges with sparkles. Then we make a huge sign.

# WELCOME HOME

We hang it across the
room. And we stick up
the picture of us all.
"It's perfect," I say
when we're done.
And it is. It really is.

**The End.**

# TINY DIAMOND!

## YOU SHINE LIKE A STAR.

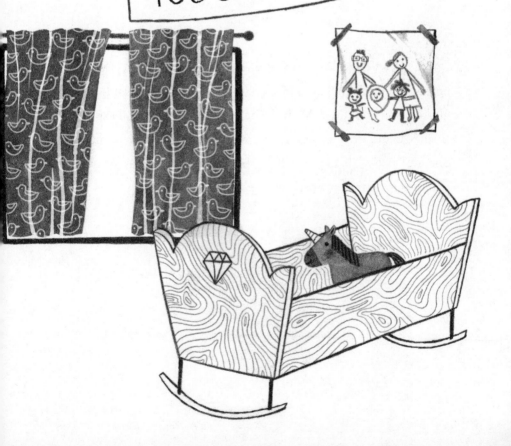

ALICE KUIPERS writes both novels and picture books. Her debut YA novel, *Life on the Refrigerator Door*, was published in thirty countries. *School Library Journal* said her debut picture book, *Violet and Victor Write the Best-Ever Bookworm Book*, was "a charming exploration of the creative process that will inspire young writers," while its sequel, *Violet and Victor Write the Most Fabulous Fairy Tale*, was a Kids' Indie Next List selection. Born in London, she now lives in Canada with her husband, who is also a writer, their four children, and their dog, Bamboo.

DIANA TOLEDANO'S name is pronounced "Deanna" because she is from Spain. Like Polly, she has curly hair and wears glasses. She grew up in Madrid where she studied art and art history. In addition to working as an illustrator, she also teaches in museums. She lives in San Francisco, where she shares a hundred-year-old house with her red-bearded husband and a fluffy kitty.